Miss Hazeltine's Home For Shy and Fearful Cats

by Alicia Potter · illustrated by Birgitta Sif

WALKER BOOKS
AND SUBSIDIARIES
LONDON · BOSTON · SYDNEY · AUCKLAND

First published in Great Britain 2015 by Walker Books Ltd
87 Vauxhall Walk, London SE11 5HJ

2 4 6 8 10 9 7 5 3 1

Text © 2015 Alicia Potter   Illustrations © 2015 Birgitta Sif

This book has been typeset in Perpetua Regular

Printed in China

British Library Cataloguing in Publication Data:
a catalogue record for this book is available from the British Library

ISBN 978-1-4063-6238-1

www.walker.co.uk

To my feral foster kittens,
who inspired this story,
and to Yodel, who stayed
~A.P.

To my purr-fect little girls,
Sóley and Salka
~B.S.

When Miss Hazeltine opened her Home for Shy and Fearful Cats, she didn't know if anyone would come.

But come they did.

"He runs from mice!"

"She's scared of birds!"

"Can't pounce!"

"Won't purr!"

"Hopeless!"

"Worthless!"

"Afraid of EVERYTHING!"

Strays who could read Miss Hazeltine's
sign skittered in on their own.
Then there was Crumb, the most timid
of all. He dashed through the door …

and hid.

Miss Hazeltine began
her lessons at once.
In the morning, she
taught Bird Basics.

In the afternoon,
Climbing Up, followed
by Climbing Down.

At night was Scary Noises.

Many cats received extra help in Meeting New Friends.

Miss Hazeltine showed the cats how to hold their tails high. To arch their backs. To think good thoughts.

Every day, they practised pouncing.

The hardest lesson?
How Not to Fear the Broom.

Miss Hazeltine didn't mind if some cats only watched. She let them be.

Like Crumb.

Miss Hazeltine told him that, sometimes, she got scared. "I'm afraid of mushrooms and owls," she confided. "And I've never liked the dark."

She praised Crumb's love of pitch-black places.

Crumb lapped up every word. One day he
hoped to find the courage to thank her.
Still, he worried. Would he ever be brave?

Soon more cats came to Miss Hazeltine's home. And
more. And more.

So many arrived that on a Monday at five o'clock, when
everyone but Crumb was fast asleep, Miss Hazeltine ran
out of milk.

"I'm off to fetch a bucketful," she told Crumb, "and will
be back before dark."

Crumb watched her go.

But by the time Miss Hazeltine rounded
the road back home, the sun had set.

The heavy buckets
sloshed and slowed her

and her ankles were wibbly-wobbly from all the pouncing. Miss Hazeltine tripped …

and fell into a ditch.

With her ankle sore and
throbbing, Miss Hazeltine was
stuck. She shivered in the dark.
The pitch-black dark. Was that
an owl hooting? She peered
around. Mushrooms!
Miss Hazeltine tried to think
good thoughts.

Back home, the cats did the same.

But they were alone — and very, very afraid.

They didn't know where Miss Hazeltine had gone!

And they hadn't yet had the lesson on What to
Do When the Lady You Love Goes Missing.

But Crumb knew where
Miss Hazeltine had gone.

And maybe, just
maybe, what to do.

Crumb stepped
into the moonlight.

He arched his back.
He held his tail high.

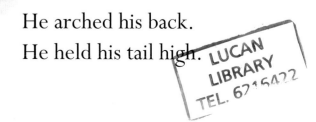

He gathered the others.
Armed with nothing but the
old broom, the residents of Miss
Hazeltine's Home for Shy and
Fearful Cats streamed into the night.

Down in the ditch, Miss Hazeltine groaned.

"What will happen to the cats?" she whispered.
"And dear, dear Crumb?"

Yet something *was* happening. The cats felt it in their chests. With Crumb leading the way, they followed the sweet smell of milk down the road ...

right to Miss Hazeltine!

At Crumb's *miaow*, the cats stared down the mushrooms.

They purred to
drown out the
owls' hoots.

And they pounced to be sure nothing lurked in the dark.

Then they formed a chain of cats to rescue
Miss Hazeltine from the ditch.
The broom made an excellent crutch.

Miss Hazeltine was escorted back to the
Home for Shy and Pretty Brave If You Ask
Us Cats (as the strays amended the sign).

"You're as bold as lions!" Miss Hazeltine told
her rescuers. "And whether you stay for
ever or head out into the world, I will never
forget your courage."
The cats were so happy that they didn't
even miss their milk.
Especially Crumb …

who had found a new favourite spot.